If I'm Not Me, Then Who Am I ?!

Afshin Tajian

Author's Note

Persian Jews, part of the Mizrahi community (Jews of West Asia), have a rich 2,700-year history in Iran/Persia. Vibrant Jewish communities once flourished in cities like Yazd, Isfahan, and Shiraz. Yazd was known for centuries as "Little Jerusalem" due to its devoted Jewish population and emphasis on religious education. Today, these cities still contain ancient, silent synagogues and Torah scrolls.

Living as a minority for centuries, Persian Jews developed a unique culture reflecting their hopes, dreams, disappointments, and achievements while maintaining their distinct identity. This heritage included stories, songs, linguistic expressions, music, and ceremonies - rooted in both Jewish values and local traditions. These cultural elements captured the spirit of a community balancing life within a different religious majority while preserving their Jewish heritage.

Haim the Giant (Haim Ghoul) emerges from the Jewish folklore of Yazd province. These oral stories, passed down through generations but never before written down, feature Haim - a simple, childlike man with a large physique. Whether Haim was based on a real person or is entirely fictional remains a mystery.

Though Haim's tales bring laughter, they often contain deeper wisdom. "If I'm Not Me, Then Who Am I?" explores identity - a universal human question that resonates especially with those living as minorities. Through Haim's innocent journey, readers of all ages discover that our true selves come from within, not from how others see us or where we find ourselves.

In a village tiny, lived Haim so grand,
With a giant's frame, but a child's playful hand.

He'd laugh and leap with joyful sound,
Like a pup at play on grassy ground.

Villagers would join in his merry play,
Laughing at his antics throughout the day.

They loved his company, his spirit so bright,
Haim's joyful presence was their delight!

Hey Haim,
do you know why the moon is round?,
It's a giant cheese wheel, high off the ground!
Mice nibble its edges each starry night,
That's why it glows with a milky light!

He wandered through villages, both near and far,
With colorful fabrics piled high on his cart.

Selling his cloth with a smile so wide,
His donkey trudged patiently by his side.

When cloth was needed, Haim was their man,
They'd wait for his donkey, as long as they can.

With berries and bread, and juice so sweet,
They'd tease him with jokes that couldn't be beat.

And one day he heard...

Hey Haim, the city hosts a feast tonight,
Many folks over there want cloth so bright!
Your fabrics will catch all shoppers' eyes,
Hurry your donkey before daylight dies!

Crowds made Haim nervous, a bustling fright,
But selling his fabrics felt oh so right.

Such a grand chance, he couldn't pass by,
So off to the city, with one deep sigh.

A crowd so big, with joyful roar,
Eating, drinking, dancing for more!

They clapped and sang in merry glee,
A grand celebration, wild and free!

At first, he paused, unsure to stay,
But treats and music led the way.

He strolled around, both shy and proud,
And showed his fabrics to the crowd!

The sky grew dark, the night was deep,
Too late to travel, too tired for sleep.

The guests lay down beneath the stars,
And Haim stayed too - no need to go far!

11

Two young men, both, sly and keen,
Spotted Haim and shared a grin.

They knew his ways, so full of cheer,
A plan for fun soon did appear!

12

Hey Haim, look here, so many sleep tight,
When morning comes, what a strange sight!
How will you know which one is truly you?
You might get mixed - what will you do?

13

Haim paused and thought, his face unsure,
Their puzzling words he couldn't ignore.

A worry grew, both deep and true,
"What if they're right - what should I do?"

I'll help you tie this pumpkin tight,
So when you wake with morning light,
You'll spot it fast and know it's you,
Not someone else, but Haim true!

15

He took their word with simple trust,
The pumpkin tied, as they discussed.

With peaceful sigh, he closed his eyes,
And slept beneath the starry skies.

They tiptoed back with sneaky glee,
Untied the pumpkin, so quietly.

To another man's leg, they tied it tight,
Then slipped away into the night.

Haim woke up at the break of day,
Ready to leave and be on his way.

But first, he checked - was he still *Haim*?
And what he found felt like a weird game!

The pumpkin was gone - no, there's no way!
Tied to another man where he slept away.

His eyes went wide, his face turned white,
Had he become someone else overnight?!

If I am truly me, where's my pumpkin, dear?
If he's the real me, then who am I here?
Am I someone else, or we are now the same?
Who's the true Haim in this curious game?!
19

Hello, excuse me, for making you awake,
I've got a question, for goodness' sake!
You wouldn't happen, to be the same,
As someone called Haim, is that your name?

"What nonsense!" growled the sleepy man,
"I'm not this Haim! Now understand?"

"Then I must be Haim!" he replied with glee,
"Relief at last - I'm still just me!"

He pondered deep, the night's strange play,
And found his truth, in morning's ray.

No pumpkin's needed, to make it so,
Haim is Haim, wherever he would go!

22

THE END